A Note to Parents and Caregivers:

Read-it! Joke Books are for children who are moving ahead on the amazing road to reading. These fun books support the acquisition and extension of reading skills as well as a love of books.

Published by the same company that produces *Read-it!* Readers, these books introduce the question/answer and dialogue patterns that help children expand their thinking about language structure and book formats.

When sharing joke books with a child, read in short stretches. Pause often to talk about the meaning of the jokes. The question/answer and dialogue formats work well for this purpose and provide an opportunity to talk about the language and meaning of the jokes. Have the child turn the pages and point to the pictures and familiar words. When you read the jokes, have fun creating the voices of characters or emphasizing some important words. Be sure to reread favorite jokes.

There is no right or wrong way to share books with children. Find time to read with your child, and pass on the legacy of literacy.

Adria F. Klein, Ph.D.
Professor Emeritus
California State University
San Bernardino, California

Editor: Christianne Jones
Designer: Joe Anderson
Page Production: Melissa Kes
Art Director: Keith Griffin
Managing Editor: Catherine Neitge
The illustrations in this book were prepared digitally.

Picture Window Books
5115 Excelsior Boulevard
Suite 232
Minneapolis, MN 55416
877-845-8392
www.picturewindowbooks.com

Printed in the United States of America.

Library of Congress Cataloging-in-Publication Data
Ziegler, Mark, 1954-
Lunchbox laughs : a book of food jokes / written by Mark Ziegler;
illustrated by Anne Haberstroh.
p. cm. – (Read-it! joke books–supercharged!)
ISBN 1-4048-0963-5
1. Food–Juvenile humor. 2. Riddles, Juvenile. I. Haberstroh, Anne.
II. Title. III. Series.

PN6231.F66Z54 2004
818'.602–dc22   2004018435

Lunchbox Laughs

A Book of Food Jokes

By Mark Ziegler • Illustrated by Anne Haberstroh

Reading Advisers:

Adria F. Klein, Ph.D.
Professor Emeritus, California State University
San Bernardino, California

Susan Kesselring, M.A., Literacy Educator
Rosemount-Apple Valley-Eagan (Minnesota) School District

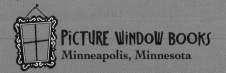

PICTURE WINDOW BOOKS
Minneapolis, Minnesota

Why did the cookie go to the doctor?

It was feeling crummy.

Why didn't the
teddy bear eat
dessert?

It was stuffed.

Why did the piecrust go
to the dentist?

It needed a filling.

What do ghosts eat
for dessert?

Ice scream!

Why is corn such a friendly vegetable?

Because it's always willing to lend an ear.

What food stays hot in the refrigerator?

Salsa.

What is a boxer's favorite drink?

Punch.

Why don't eggs tell jokes?

They'd crack each other up.

What did the farmer plant
in his sofa?

Couch potatoes.

How do you make a casserole?

Put it on roller skates.

What did the soda say to the bottle opener?

"Can you help me find my Pop?"

Why are strawberries such bad drivers?

They always get stuck in a jam.

Why did the waitress walk all over the pizza?

Because the customer told her to step on it!

Where do bakers keep
their dough?

In the bank.

What did the plate say to
the tablecloth?

"Lunch is on me."

What kind of lunch does a
cheetah eat?

Fast food.

What kind of fruit
is never lonely?

Pears.

What did the hot dog say when it crossed the finish line?

"I'm the wiener!"

Why did the orange
lose the race?

It ran out of juice.

What do you use to
fix a broken ketchup
bottle?

Tomato paste.

What did the astronaut put in
his sandwich?

Launch meat.

Why didn't the raisin go to
the dance?

It couldn't find a date.

What do frogs eat with their hamburgers?

French flies.

Why did the little cookie cry?

His mother had been a wafer so long.

What vegetable do you get when an elephant walks through your garden?

Squash.

Why couldn't the monkey eat the banana?

Because the banana split.

What do cheerleaders drink before a game?

Root beer!

Where do smart hot dogs end up?

On the honor roll.

Why did the doughnut maker sell his store?

He was tired of the hole business.

Why did the student eat her homework?

The teacher told her it was a piece of cake.

What did the gingerbread boy use to make his bed?

Cookie sheets.

What is the worst kind of cake to have?

A stomach-cake.

Why did the boy stare at the can of orange juice?

It said concentrate.

Why did the sesame seeds get dizzy?

They were on a roll.

What is the best thing to take before a meal?

A seat!

How is a baseball team like a pancake?

They both need a good batter.

Why do crazy people like to eat cashews?

Because they're nuts!

How many rotten eggs does it take to stink up a kitchen?

Quite a phew!

What kind of food is good for your eyes?

Seafood.

Why did the banana make
so many friends?

Because he had a peel.

How do strawberries greet each other?

Strawberries shake.

What do you get when you cross a cow with a duck?

Milk and quackers.

What did the hamburgers name their daughter?

Patty.

What do porcupines like to put on their hamburgers?

Sweet prickles.

What kind of shoes can you make from bananas?

Slippers.

Read-it! Joke Books— Supercharged!

Beastly Laughs: A Book of Monster Jokes by Michael Dahl

Chalkboard Chuckles: A Book of Classroom Jokes by Mark Moore

Creepy Crawlers: A Book of Bug Jokes by Mark Moore

Critter Jitters: A Book of Animal Jokes by Mark Ziegler

Giggle Bubbles: A Book of Underwater Jokes by Mark Ziegler

Goofballs! A Book of Sports Jokes by Mark Ziegler

Lunchbox Laughs: A Book of Food Jokes by Mark Ziegler

Roaring with Laughter: A Book of Animal Jokes by Michael Dahl

School Kidders: A Book of School Jokes by Mark Ziegler

Sit! Stay! Laugh! A Book of Pet Jokes by Michael Dahl

Spooky Sillies: A Book of Ghost Jokes by Mark Moore

Wacky Wheelies: A Book of Transportation Jokes by Mark Ziegler

Looking for a specific title or level? A complete list
of *Read-it!* Readers is available on our Web site:
www.picturewindowbooks.com